D0088890

Published by
ARCHAIA™

Written by

Aline Brosh McKenna

Illustrated by

Ramón K. Pérez

Colored by

Irma Kniivila

with Ramón K. Pérez

Lettered by

Deron Bennett

Inspired by *Jane Eyre* by

Charlotte Brontë

I ♥ NY

Cover by
Ramón K. Pérez

Designer
Jillian Crab

Associate Editor
Cameron Chittock

Editor
Sierra Hahn

Special Thanks to Stephen Christy, Rebecca Taylor, Dafna Pleban, Elizabeth Bubriski, Ilana Peña, Alden Derck, and Scott Newman.

BOOM! Studios, 5670 Wilshire Boulevard, Suite 450, Los Angeles, CA 90036-5679. Printed in Canada. First Printing.

ISBN: 978-1-60886-981-7, eISBN: 978-1-61398-652-3

For Charlotte Brontë, who withstood
great loss with great dignity.

—Aline Brosh McKenna

We all have our journey, the story we are the star of. Here you hold Jane's, but it is also a part of mine. I'd like to thank my Mama and Papa for setting the foundation with their support, giving me the opportunity, but allowing me the freedom to build the stage, create the show, play the music, light the lights, and raise the curtain on the most sensational, inspirational, celebrational...well, you get the idea. Dziękuję, gracias, and thank you. I love you both.

—Ramón K. Pérez

My parents worked on the water.

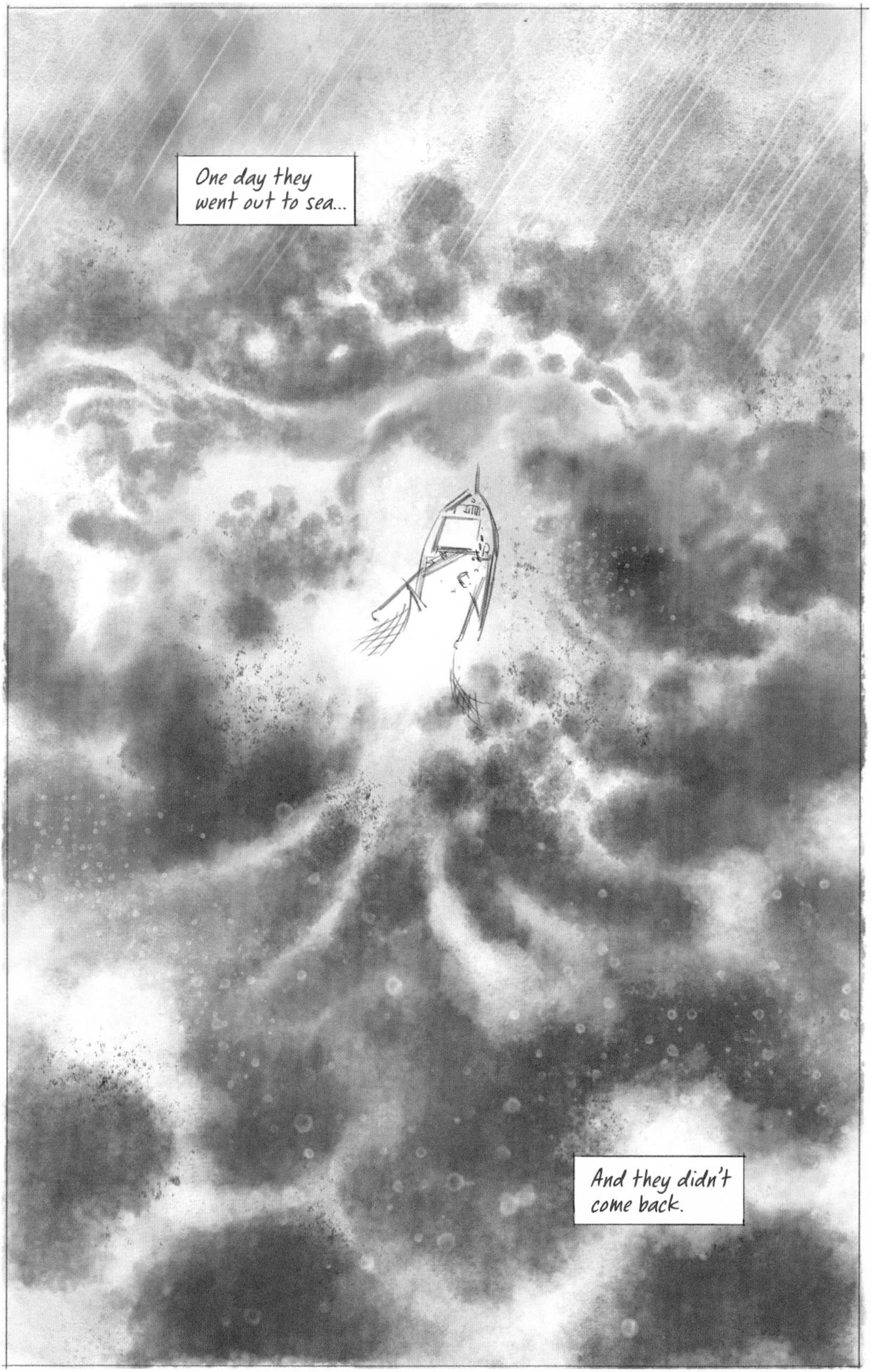

One day they went out to sea...

And they didn't come back.

My aunt and my cousins lived two towns over. My mother wasn't close to her sister. I didn't know them well.
But I had nowhere else to go.
37

Living there was not living. I was biding my time.
I always knew I didn't belong.
I learned to be invisible.

Most of the time I felt like I didn't belong anywhere.
No one had any use for me. But I knew I could do one thing.
I could take what I saw and put it on a piece of paper.

I hoped one day THAT would be my ticket out. In the meantime, I had to earn money.
I found work.
I went out on as many trips as I could.
Saved every single penny I earned.

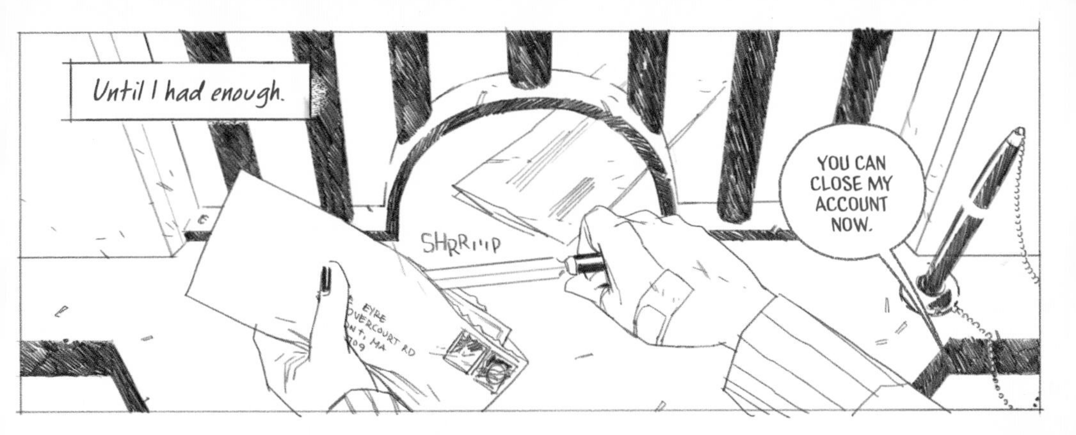

I knew there was a wide world out there, as big as the ocean. All I needed was the courage to go.

There were things I could have said. About how I had been treated. About how I could never, ever come back. Instead, I left there the same way I had lived there.

BUS TERMINAL

NYC
BZZZT
JANE?

YEP, THAT'S ME.
I'M HECTOR.
YOU GOT HERE OKAY?
YEAH. GREAT NEIGHBORHOOD.

DURING THE DAY, IT'S PRETTY SAFE. AT NIGHT, YOU GOTTA BE CAREFUL.
HMM. YOU DIDN'T MENTION THAT IN YOUR AD.

WOULD *YOU*?

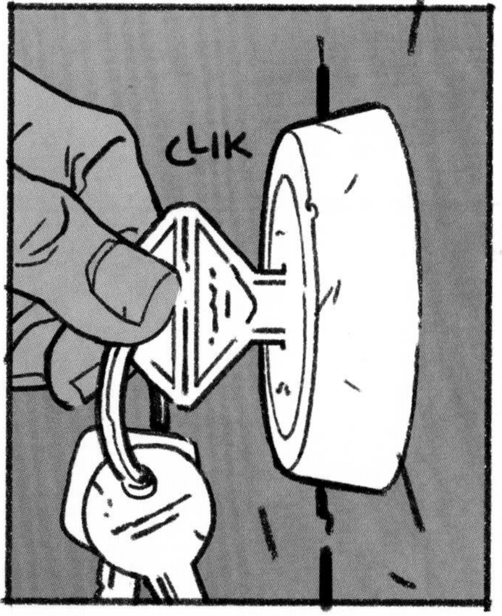
CLIK

COME ON IN.
The whole apartment could've fit on the deck of a fishing boat.

But to me, it was heaven.
HERE WE HAVE MY SEWING ROOM, LIVING ROOM, DINING ROOM ALL IN ONE!

THIS CLOTHING IS BEAUTIFUL.

THANKS. I'LL LEND YOU ONE OF MY PIECES ONE DAY.

OKAY! I'VE NEVER WORN A "PIECE," BUT SURE!

SOFA. TV. THE BASICS.

BATHROOM... WHERE'S THE REST OF YOUR STUFF? I HAVE A VAN, I COULD HELP YOU.
NOPE, THIS IS IT.

WOW. FRUGAL. SO, YOU'RE AN ARTIST?

NOT YET. MAYBE SOMEDAY.

WHAT KIND OF WORK DO YOU DO?
WELL, I WORKED ON A FISHING BOAT FOR THE LAST COUPLE--
OH, MY WORK. WELL, I DON'T KNOW HOW TO DESCRIBE IT. I GUESS I JUST--
HERE IT IS. "ALCOVE" SOUNDED BETTER THAN "PANTRY" IN THE AD.
--DRAW WHAT I SEE...

CLICK

My first subway ride.
I was overwhelmed.

So much life to draw.

The art students waiting to register were the coolest people I'd ever seen.

YOU'LL NEED TO FIND A JOB BY THE END OF THE WEEK TO MAINTAIN YOUR SCHOLARSHIP.
END OF THE WEEK? BUT I JUST GOT HERE--
MOST OF THE STUDENTS GET HERE A WEEK EARLY TO LINE SOMETHING UP.
"LISTINGS ARE IN THE CAREER CENTER. THEY GOT ALL KINDS OF STUFF THERE.
ORBIT HIRING
Ideal applicants exhibit a passion for punctuality and modesty. We are seeking highly qualified candidates who can act with the utmost level of discretion and professionalism. Interested applications should submit their resumes through Career Center portal.
please submit resumes via the Career Center portal.
RICARDO'S VINTAGE WEAR
A love of fashion is a must.
vintage items. If allergies are
please do not apply. Contact can be
their resumes
portal.
"GET A JOB AND GET THIS SIGNED."

BUT WHAT KIND OF JOB IS IT?
THE LISTING WASN'T VERY SPECIFIC, BUT IT PAYS WELL AND IT SAYS I CAN START IMMEDIATELY.

THIS GOOD?
YOU HAVE ANYTHING ELSE?

...
THEN I **LOVE** IT.

The city was an endless maze.

I would have to find my own way.
NYC TAXI

Somehow.
DING

MISS--
HI, I BROUGHT A RESUME, I--
WE CHECKED YOU OUT ALREADY.
WAIT, WHAT?
YOU CLEARED. SO YOU'RE HIRED. WE NEED SOMEONE RIGHT AWAY. BIT OF A STAFFING CRISIS.
DISCRETION IS AN ABSOLUTE PREREQUISITE OF THE JOB.
N.D.A. NON DISCLOSURE AGREEMENT.
YOU DON'T TWEET, FACEBOOK, INSTAGRAM, SNAPCHAT, WHATSAPP--
I DON'T EVEN KNOW WHAT HALF THOSE THINGS ARE.
...OR YOU WILL BE TERMINATED AND SUED.
BUT WHAT'S THE JOB, EXACTLY? I DON'T KNOW IF I'M QUALIFIED--
THERE ARE OTHER APPLICANTS. ARE YOU INTERESTED?
SIGNING!
TERRIFIC. THE ADDRESS WILL BE EMAILED TO YOU.

I LOOKED THE ADDRESS UP.
THE BUILDING HAS MORE BILLIONAIRES THAN THE REST OF THE UNITED STATES COMBINED. LAST YEAR AN APARTMENT SOLD FOR...

70 MILLION DOLLARS.
HECTOR, I CAN'T WORK THERE. I DON'T KNOW ANYTHING ABOUT THAT WORLD, THOSE PEOPLE, I'M GONNA STICK OUT LIKE A--

HEY, DON'T COMPLAIN-- A JOB'S A JOB!

"AND YOU NEED ONE BY FRIDAY, REMEMBER?"

740
MAGDA IS EXPECTING YOU.
DING

DING

UM... HELLO?

I'M JANE.

YOU MUST BE...
MAGDA.

BIG PLACE.
SO WHAT KIND OF JOB WOULD I BE--

I THINK YOU SHOULD KNOW THAT THE LAST ONE ONLY MADE IT A WEEK.
THE LAST WHAT?

DOES THIS WOMAN LIVE HERE?

UH... MAGDA?

TOK

TRRRLLLLL

YOU TOOK MY MONEY.

THAT'S MY QUARTER. GIVE IT BACK OR I'LL TELL MAGDA YOU'RE A STEALER.

AND YOU ARE...?

YOU DON'T KNOW WHY YOU'RE HERE? OKAY. MY MOM IS DEAD. MY DAD IS ALWAYS OUT OF TOWN, I BARELY SEE HIM. YOU'RE MY NANNY.

AH. I SEE, OKAY.
NOW CAN I HAVE MY QUARTER?
I'M GOING TO KEEP THIS QUARTER. BUT I'LL LET YOU EARN IT BACK.

I'VE NEVER BEEN HERE BEFORE. IF YOU SHOW ME AROUND, THE APARTMENT, I WILL PAY YOU EXACTLY 25 CENTS.
The only thing I had ever taken care of before was fish in a bucket, but how hard could it be?

SO, UM... WHAT DOES YOUR DAD DO?
DUNNO.

C'MON!

WE DON'T EAT DINNER HERE BUT IT'S PRETTY.

WHEN MAGDA'S NOT LOOKING I SLIDE DOWN THAT BANNISTER...YOU COULD TRY.
ANOTHER TIME, MAYBE!

THAT'S BILL. HE MAKES THE BEST COOKIES.

SEE?

DON'T TELL MAGDA?
DEAL.

DAD LIKES BOOKS. LOTS OF THEM. SOMETIMES HE READS ALL NIGHT.

ALL NIGHT?

DADDY'S OFFICE IS DOWN THERE.

COME SEE THE VIEW!

WOW.

I felt an immediate connection to her. A lonely kid is a lonely kid.

YOU SEE THAT DOOR? THAT DOOR GOES UPSTAIRS. DON'T GO UP THERE OR TRY THE DOOR OR ASK TO GO UP THERE OR ANYTHING LIKE THAT, OKAY?
NINE DIFFERENT NANNIES GOT FIRED BECAUSE THEY TRIED THE DOOR.
NINE? HOW MANY HAVE YOU HAD?
ELEVENTY.

HIS NAME IS EDWARD ROCHESTER. HE'S A PARTNER OF ONE OF THE BIGGEST HEDGE FUNDS IN THE COUNTRY, ORBIT FUNDS. IT'S HIS WIFE'S FAMILY'S FUND. HE RUNS IT WITH HER BROTHER, RICHARD MASON.

WHOA. IT SAYS HERE HIS WIFE, ISABEL "WAS KILLED IN AN ATTEMPTED MUGGING IN 2012, LEAVING BEHIND A DAUGHTER, ADELE."
OH, SO SAD.

WHAT DOES HE LOOK LIKE? I'M GOING TO NEED TO SEE A PICTURE BEFORE I CAN FIGURE OUT IF I'M INTERESTED IN THIS WHOLE THING.

ALL I COULD FIND WAS THIS.

DARK, HANDSOME, AND BLURRY. JUST YOUR TYPE!
HE SEEMS TO GO TO A LOT OF PARTIES AND DATE A LOT OF WOMEN.
WHAT HAVE I GOTTEN MYSELF INTO?

IT'S IMPORTANT TO KNOW WHO YOU ARE.
...IF YOU DON'T KNOW **WHO YOU ARE,** YOU CAN NEVER EXPRESS YOUR UNIQUE TAKE ON ART, YOUR IDIOSYNCRATIC VOICE.

PSST... HEY, HI, I'M NICOLE...

MS. EYRE, DID YOU HEAR WHAT I JUST SAID? ABOUT EXPRESSING YOUR INDIVIDUALITY?

YOU'RE AN INTERPRETER, NOT A CAMERA. REMEMBER THAT.

BUT THAT'S... HOW I SEE THINGS.

SHRIIIP

IGNORE CHANTAL, OKAY? SHE'S A BITCH. COUPLE YEARS MAKING PISS SCULPTURES FOR DAMIEN HIRST AND YOU THINK YOU'RE A GENIUS.

OKAY, THANK YOU.
WE'RE GOING TO GET COFFEE AT ONE OF THE INSUFFERABLE, OVERPRICED PLACES AROUND THE CORNER. YOU INTERESTED? IT'S ON MY DAD'S CREDIT CARD.

OH, THAT'S... SO NICE OF YOU, BUT I HAVE TO GO TO WORK. RAIN CHECK, OKAY?

DO I MAKE A LEFT HERE?

A RIGHT.
UM, THANKS...
...TELL ME YOUR NAME AGAIN?

...
IF YOU'RE GOING TO BE PROTECTING ME AND ADELE...

I WANT TO CALL YOU SOMETHING...

I'LL CALL YOU STEVE, OKAY?

AND WE'RE SURE THAT A MASSIVE BODYGUARD IS NOT OVERKILL FOR THE FIRST GRADE PICKUP RUN?

The school building was fancier than any place in my hometown.

YOU ARE HERE FOR...
ADELE?
NEW NANNY...HAVEN'T SEEN HER DAD IN MONTHS...POOR GIRL...

YOU'RE HERE!
OF COURSE I'M HERE.
POOF

NOW, WHAT DO YOU DO AFTER SCHOOL?
GO HOME.
AND WHAT DO YOU DO THERE?
NOTHING.
YEAH, THAT'S NOT GONNA WORK.

WHERE DO ALL YOUR FRIENDS LIVE? AROUND HERE?
DUNNO.

SOMETIMES PEOPLE GO THERE FOR BREAKFAST BEFORE SCHOOL. NOT ME. OTHER KIDS. WITH THEIR MOMS. THEY HAVE WAFFLES. I CAN SEE IT THROUGH THE WINDOW.
ALICE'S TEA CUP
CAFE
ALICE'S TEA CUP

WHERE ARE WE GOING?
ALICE'S TEA CUP
CAFE

LISTEN, STEVE.
WE'RE DOING FINE HERE, IF YOU WANT TO GET A COFFEE OR SOMETHING OR--

HIGHER!
MY NAME IS NOT STEVE.

TODAY WAS FUN. BUT IT'S OKAY IF YOU DON'T COME BACK.
THAT HAPPENS SOMETIMES. AND IT'S ONLY BEEN ONE DAY.
ADELE--
IT'S WEIRD HERE. I KNOW THAT. I KNOW IT'S SPOOKY AND WEIRD HERE.

"WHAT? NO, IT ISN'T."

CREAK

MAGDA! THERE WAS A...
CLICK

THERE WAS A MAN AND HE WENT UP THOSE STAIRS. IS THAT ADELE'S FATHER?
WAIT!

I NEED TO TALK TO HIM.
IF I'M GOING TO BE TAKING CARE OF ADELE, I NEED TO TELL HIM WHAT'S GOING ON WITH HER--
THAT'S NOT HIM.

Did Adele even have a father? Maybe he was just a ghost.

Just when it seemed like the day couldn't get weirder.

HFF
HFF

RESEARCH ASSISTANT, AVAILABLE IMMEDIATELY

University Archives is seeking a research assistant to aid in the maintenance and cataloguing of our extensive library. This position consists mostly of data entry and requires intense focus and attention to detail. Shifts begin at 6pm and last until 11pm submit resumes and weekly availability through the Career Portal.

"I HAVE TO FIND A DIFFERENT JOB."

CLIK

RESEARCH ASSIS

Univer Archives

loguing o ur exten

intense focus and a

submit resumes and

MISS.
DING
YOU'RE HERE TOO EARLY.
I NEED TO TALK TO MR. ROCHESTER.
HE'S BUSY.
I'LL WAIT.
THE LAST ONE MADE IT A WEEK. YOU, A DAY. YOU MUST BE VERY PROUD OF YOURSELF.
JANE?

ADELE! YOU SCARED ME.
IT'S SO EARLY, GO BACK TO SLEEP--

IT'S OKAY. I TOLD YOU THIS MIGHT HAPPEN. DON'T FEEL BAD.

YOU NEEDED TO TALK TO ME?

There he was.
Dark, handsome,
and NOT blurry.

I was NOT going to let him scare me. No way.

YES. I NEED TO TELL YOU SOMETHING IMPORTANT.

WE WANT TO GO OUT TO BREAKFAST.

BEFORE SCHOOL. WAFFLES.

THAT'S WHY YOU ARE BOTHERING ME?

TEA CUP
BRUNCH
ALICE'S TEA

I stayed for Adele. I couldn't abandon her.
TEA CUP

I would try to make this work.

BOOP

HI.
HELLO.
NEW NANNY?
YES, I--
AH YES, THEY COME AND THEY GO.

RICHARD MASON. I'M ROCHESTER'S BROTHER-IN-LAW. BUSINESS PARTNER. ADELE'S UNCLE.
I KNOW WHO YOU ARE. I'M JANE. EYRE.

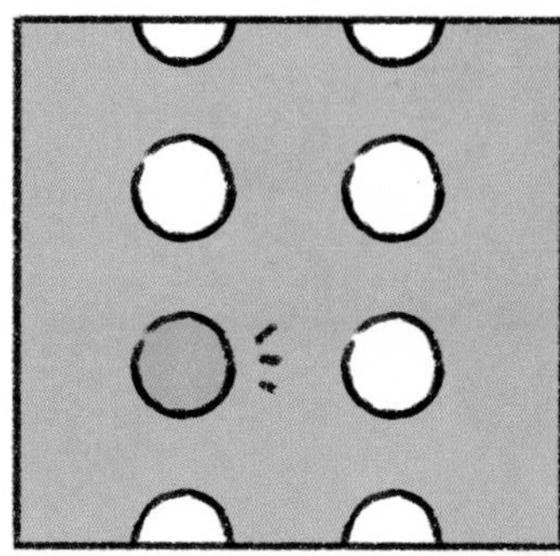

HE BEING A JERK?
ROCHESTER, HE CAN BE A REAL PAIN. I MEAN, I LOVE THE GUY, BUT--

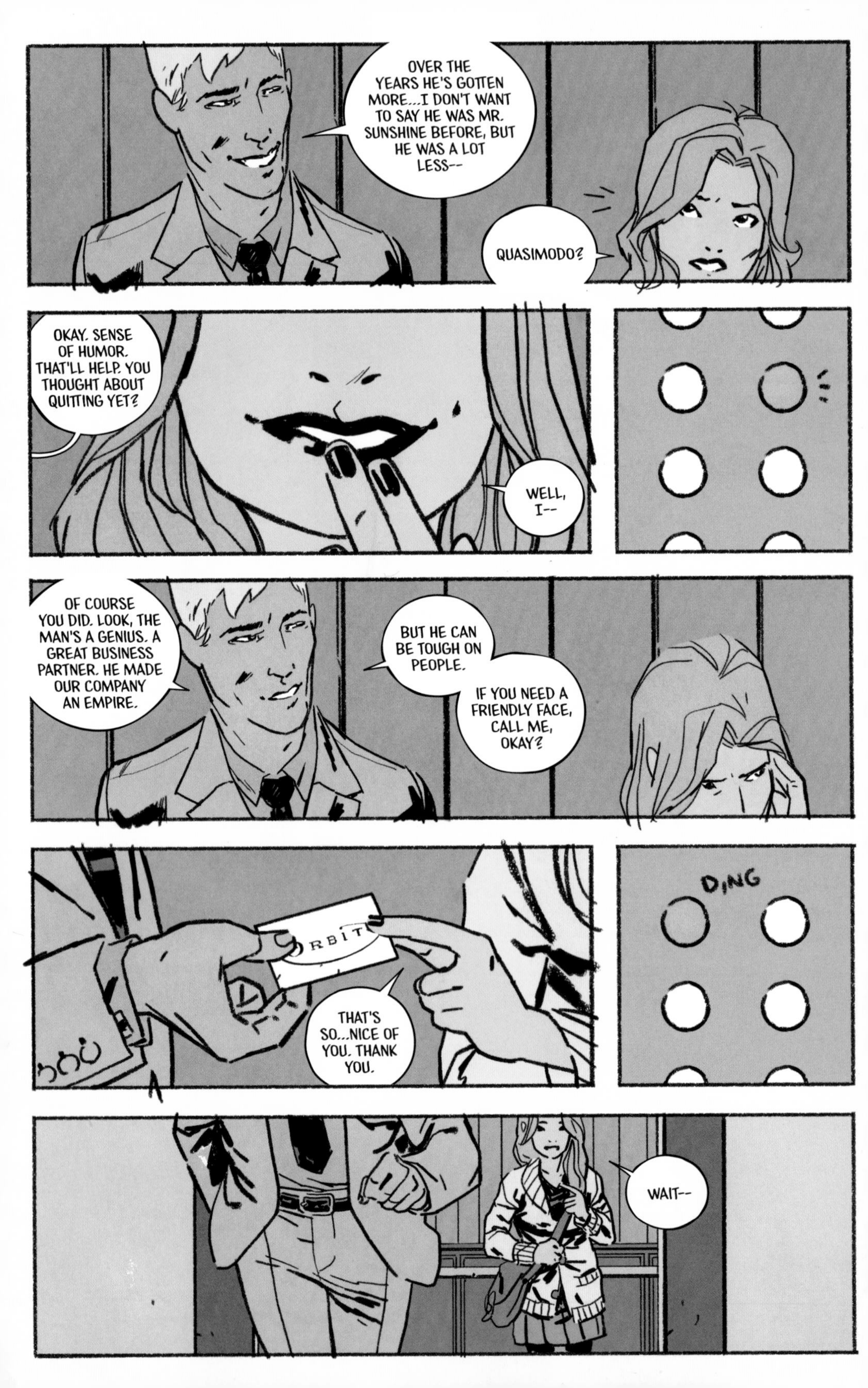
OVER THE YEARS HE'S GOTTEN MORE...I DON'T WANT TO SAY HE WAS MR. SUNSHINE BEFORE, BUT HE WAS A LOT LESS--
QUASIMODO?
OKAY. SENSE OF HUMOR. THAT'LL HELP. YOU THOUGHT ABOUT QUITTING YET?
WELL, I--
OF COURSE YOU DID. LOOK, THE MAN'S A GENIUS. A GREAT BUSINESS PARTNER. HE MADE OUR COMPANY AN EMPIRE.
BUT HE CAN BE TOUGH ON PEOPLE.
IF YOU NEED A FRIENDLY FACE, CALL ME, OKAY?
RBIT
THAT'S SO...NICE OF YOU. THANK YOU.
DING
WAIT--

ACTUALLY, I COULD USE YOUR HELP. I HAVE SOMETHING TO TELL HIM. AND I DON'T THINK HE'S GOING TO LIKE IT.
ARE YOU **RIGHT?**
THE THING YOU WANT TO TELL HIM, ARE YOU RIGHT ABOUT IT?

THEN COME WITH ME.

Out of nowhere, I had an ally in Mason.

ARE YOU READY?

SO, UM...MR. ROCHESTER, I NEED TO TALK TO YOU.
ABOUT ADELE.
SHE'S HAVING PROBLEMS.

IN SCHOOL.

IT'S THE BEST SCHOOL IN THE CITY.

SO? HOW DOES THAT MATTER?
SHE HAS NO FRIENDS. NO SOCIAL LIFE. NOT INVITED TO ANY PARTIES. SHE NEVER SPEAKS UP IN CLASS, SO SHE FALLS BEHIND AND THEY DON'T NOTICE--

GET HER A TUTOR THEN.

THE TEACHERS SAY IT'S BEEN GOING ON FOR MONTHS. SOMEONE NEEDS TO DO SOMETHING. I DON'T KNOW MUCH ABOUT A LOT OF THINGS, BUT I KNOW WHEN A KID NEEDS HELP.
SO, I, UM, GOT YOU AN APPOINTMENT WITH HER TEACHERS.

WHAT? I'M NOT GOING TO--

I HAVE ANOTHER GOOD JOB. AT THE RESEARCH LIBRARY. I ALREADY APPLIED AND GOT IT. I WOULD LIKE TO HELP ADELE, BUT I CAN'T DO IT ON MY OWN. IF YOU WON'T DO THIS, I QUIT.

WHO THE HELL ARE YOU AGAIN?

SOMEONE WHO WAS ALSO A LONELY KID.

When I was a kid,
no one had ever
spoken up for me.
I knew I had to
speak up for Adele
No matter how
he reacted.
So...
11 A.M.
ON THE
16TH.

I couldn't believe it.
CLICK

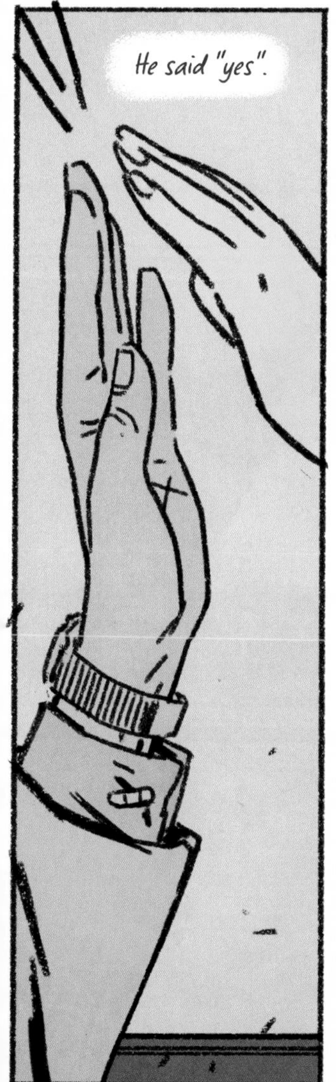
He said "yes".

THANK YOU.

DON'T THANK ME.

IT WAS ENTIRELY YOU, JANE EYRE.

PLOOF
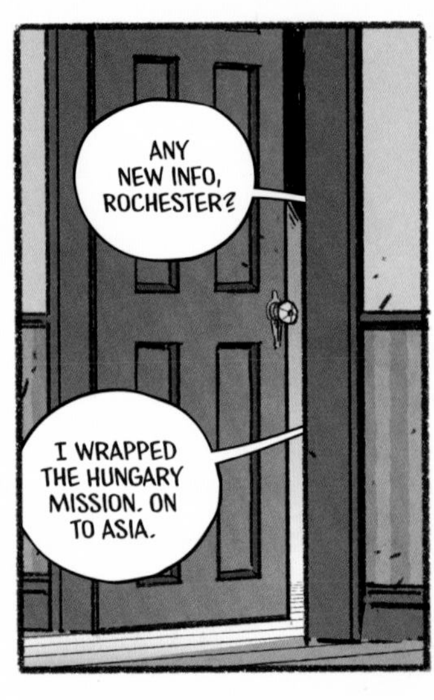
ANY NEW INFO, ROCHESTER?
I WRAPPED THE HUNGARY MISSION. ON TO ASIA.

THAT'S MY CUE TO GO!

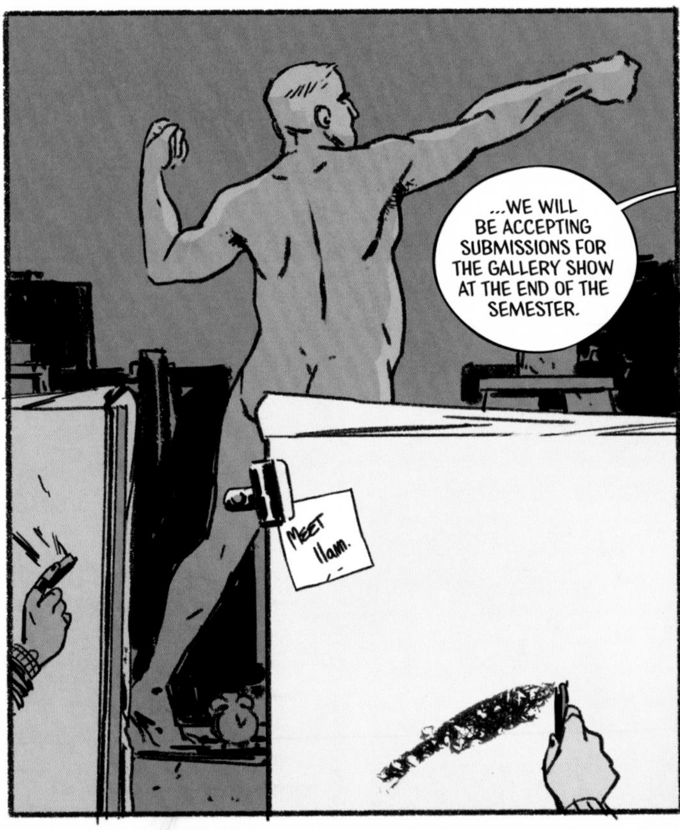
...WE WILL BE ACCEPTING SUBMISSIONS FOR THE GALLERY SHOW AT THE END OF THE SEMESTER.
MEET 11am.

WE TAKE VERY LITTLE OF THE WORK SUBMITTED, ONLY ABOUT TEN PERCENT...
APPT 11 AM

MISS EYRE, YOU HAVE SOMEWHERE BETTER TO BE?
NOPE.

DAMMIT--
APPT 11 AM

YOU REMINDED HIM, RIGHT MAGDA?

I ASKED YOU TO PUT IT IN HIS CALENDAR.

The other nannies were huddled, gossiping.

It was like they had seen a ghost. Which, in a way, they had.

Aa Bb Cc Dd Ee Ff
WE TRY NOT TO INTERVENE IN PLAYGROUND DYNAMICS. SO IMPORTANT IN ESTABLISHING SELF-ESTEEM.
OH, WOULD YOU LISTEN TO YOURSELF? THAT'S A BUNCH OF BABBLE.

BUT SHE'S A NICE KID. AND SHE'S SMART, I KNOW SHE IS.

WE HAD AN ITALIAN BABY-SITTER WHEN SHE WAS THREE AND SHE LEARNED HOW TO SAY "THANK YOU," "I'M SORRY," AND "LET'S GO SHOPPING," IN ITALIAN.

MR. ROCHESTER, THANK YOU FOR COMING--

OH, DON'T THANK ME. I BARELY DO ANYTHING AS A FATHER. YOU KNOW THAT BETTER THAN ANYONE.
STILL. THANK YOU.

I MEANT WHAT I SAID, BY THE WAY.

THE THING YOU OVERHEARD WHEN YOU WERE EAVESDROPPING. I HAVE NO IDEA HOW THE HELL WE FOUND YOU, BUT ADELE IS LUCKY TO HAVE YOU.

OH, AND SORRY I SPLASHED YOU WITH MY CAR THE OTHER NIGHT.

Was he decent or terrible? I couldn't figure it out.
VROOM

But I knew who to ask.
McKENNA'S
DIDN'T THINK YOU WOULD CALL.

ME NEITHER. THANK YOU FOR COMING. SO...YOUR SISTER ISABEL, SHE WAS SO BEAUTIFUL.
YES, SHE WAS. ALWAYS. SHE AND ROCHESTER MET IN COLLEGE AND THEY JUST...FUSED. I'D NEVER SEEN HER LIKE THAT.

WOW. TRUE LOVE, HUH?

AFTER THEY GOT MARRIED, THEY TOOK TRIPS. THE ATTACK HAPPENED ON ONE OF THEM...SHE NEVER CAME HOME. ROCHESTER FELL APART. WE ALL DID. BUT HE WENT FULL HUNCHBACK.

OH, MASON, THAT'S TERRIBLE!

I CAN TELL HE LOVES ADELE. AND I FEEL BAD FOR BOTH OF THEM.
IT'S JUST A REALLY WEIRD WORKPLACE.

OH GOD, NOW I CAN'T STOP PICTURING HIM RINGING THE BELLS OF NOTRE DAME!
YOU'RE THE BEST THING TO HAPPEN TO THEM SINCE ISABEL. CHEERS TO THE BRAVE, MS. EYRE.

DID I EVER TELL YOU WHAT HAPPENED TO MY MOM?
SHE WAS A FAIRY PRINCESS. SHE GOT SENT BACK TO HER MAGICAL LAND. SHE DIDN'T WANNA GO, BUT THEY MADE HER.
YEAH. WHERE DOES YOUR MOM LIVE?
I'M SURE SHE MISSES YOU. A LOT.

OH, SHE DIED TOO. WHEN I WAS NOT MUCH OLDER THAN YOU.
SHE *DID*?

YOU DON'T HAVE A MOM EITHER. AND YOU'RE... OKAY?

YEAH. BASICALLY.
JANE, YOU'RE GONNA STAY HERE FOREVER, RIGHT?

GOOD NIGHT, SWEETIE.

THRUM
TOK
CLICK

THRMMM-TOK-TH
What was that?

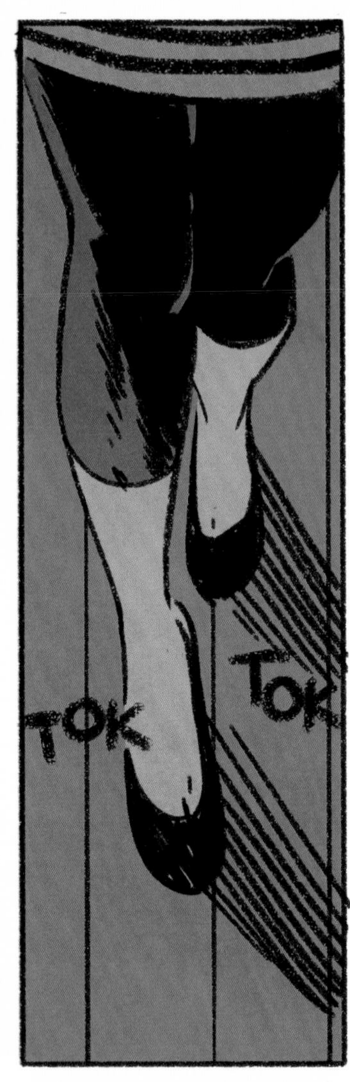
TOK
TOK

THRMMM TOK THRM
MAGDA?

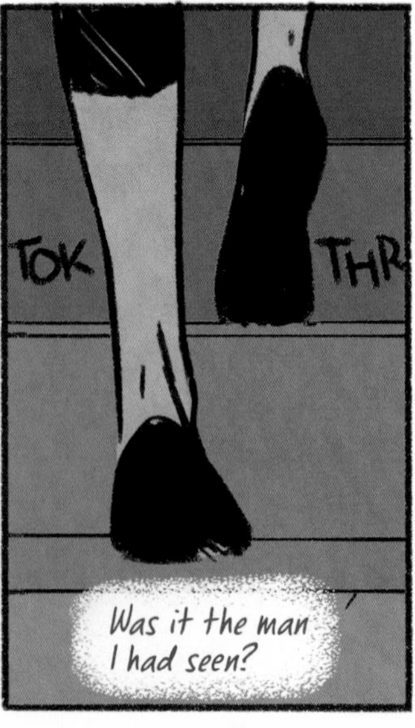
TOK
THR
Was it the man
I had seen?

THRMMM - TOK

JANE?

JANE!

HEARD YOU IN THE FRONT HALL.
YEAH, SORRY, I WAS JUST LEAVING FOR THE DAY AND THOUGHT I HEARD SOMETHING--

SIT.

TINK

WE DON'T KNOW EACH OTHER VERY WELL, DO WE?
WHERE ARE YOU FROM?

MASSACHUSETTS.
I'M SURE IT'S ALL IN MY FILE OR WHATEVER.
I DON'T READ FILES.

WHY DID YOU COME TO NEW YORK?

I WANTED A NEW LIFE.

BUT WHY HERE?

IT SEEMS LIKE A GOOD PLACE TO START OVER.

YOU KNOW, THERE IS SOMETHING ABOUT YOU.

SOMETHING I FELT THE FIRST TIME WE MET.

YOU DON'T CARE ABOUT MONEY, OR FAME, OR WHAT PEOPLE SAY.

PEOPLE ARE USUALLY WRONG.

YOU SEE THINGS.

THAT CAN BE DANGEROUS.

THE WORLD IS A SCARY PLACE.

I'M NOT SURE IT DESERVES PEOPLE LIKE YOU.

Decent or terrible?

Maybe decent?

SORRY, I'M TALKING TOO MUCH. ME AND THE WHISKEY. YOU CAN GO.
OKAY. THANK YOU FOR YOUR TIME. AND YOUR KIND WORDS.

OH, AND JANE?

YES, SIR.

ONE LAST THING.

DON'T TOUCH THE DOOR AGAIN.

TO THE THIRD FLOOR. DON'T **EVER** DO THAT AGAIN. OKAY?

DID YOU HEAR ME?
YES, I'M SORRY.

Never mind. Terrible.

I had never felt so confused by anyone.

All I knew was that, for some reason, I could not stop drawing him.

DO YOU LIKE HIM?
MOST OF THESE, I CAN TELL HOW YOU FEEL ABOUT THE PERSON. BUT THIS ONE...THE DARK AND THE LIGHT...WHAT DO YOU THINK OF HIM?

TRULY, NO IDEA.

OKAY. WELL, I THINK HE'S HOT.

It seemed like every day he surprised me somehow.
WHERE ARE YOU GUYS GOING?

UH, THE PARK.

WHICH ONE?
YOU WANNA COME WITH US?!

SURE.

YOU AND ADELE COME HERE A LOT?
YEP.

ISABEL USED TO TAKE ADELE HERE TOO.
SHE WAS A GREAT MOTHER.

SHE WAS A GREAT... EVERYTHING.

...
YOU THINK I COULD DO THIS AGAIN? COME TO THE PARK WITH YOU GUYS?

NO, I'M SORRY, ABSOLUTELY NOT...
YOU'RE NOT A NICE PERSON.

On the outside, Rochester was different from me in every way, but there was something...some connection between us.
I couldn't explain it, but it felt like a kind of string tied to each of us, pulling us together.

When I was with him and Adele, I felt like I was home, the first real home I'd had in a long time.

I started to look forward to every day...

YOU LATE FOR SCHOOL?
WORK. WE'RE TAKING ADELE TO DINNER FOR HER HALF-BIRTHDAY.

SRSLY?

YOU KNOW THAT YOUR JOB IS...A JOB, RIGHT?
I DON'T KNOW WHAT YOU'RE TALKING ABOUT.
HOW'S SCHOOL GOING? YOU SUBMIT ANY PIECES FOR THE SHOW?
YOU DIDN'T SCALE FISH AND SAVE YOUR MONEY SO YOU COULD COME TO NEW YORK AND BE SOMEONE'S KINDA WIFE...

SEE YOU LATER, MOM.

UM, DAD, YOU EAT CHEESEBURGERS?

OF COURSE I DO. YEARS OF EATING WHITE CASTLE.
WHAT'S WHITE CASTLE? IS THAT WHERE PRINCESSES EAT?
ONLY THE FUN ONES.

HERE, LET ME.

SEE? I CAN DO THINGS.

ALICE'S TEA
CAFE · PÂTISSIER

CLIK

OH! YOU STARTLED ME.

SORRY, I WAS JUST... GOODNIGHT, JANE.

GOODNIGHT, SIR.

Days went by like this. An unusual but happy time. And then...
THE BALLET.
WHAT?

THERE IS A BIG PARTY FOR THE BALLET. MR. ROCHESTER SAYS YOU SHOULD GO WITH HIM AND ADELE.
ADELE WILL NEED SOME KIND OF DRESS. AND YOU TOO, YOU WILL HAVE TO WEAR SOMETHING--

APPROPRIATE.

OF COURSE. APPROPRIATE FOR A BALLET PARTY? THAT'S NO PROBLEM...

YOU ARE GOING TO THE OPENING OF THE AMERICAN BALLET THEATER SEASON?

CAN I WEAR THIS?
UM...
YOU SAID GALA, NOT FISH FRY.

YOU WILL BE WITH THE RICHEST, MOST INFLUENTIAL, CHICEST PEOPLE IN THE WORLD. YOU NEED A ***DRESS.*** CAPITAL D.

UH, NO ONE WILL NOTICE WHAT I'M WEARING.
MAYBE, BUT I CAN'T HAVE YOU SEEN IN PUBLIC LIKE THAT.

FASH
FASH
FASH

We were a long way from the fishing docks.

I was afraid I looked like a fool.

I hoped no one would notice how out of place I felt.
WOW. THIS IS INCREDIBLE.
THERE'S DADDY!
TIP

This time, when our eyes met...

Everything seemed different.

BALLET IS BORING, BUT ADELE LOVES THIS PARTY.

AND I HOPED YOU WOULDN'T MIND.

YOU'RE SO... YOU'RE... THANK YOU FOR COMING, JANE.

If he thought
this was boring.

What was
exciting?

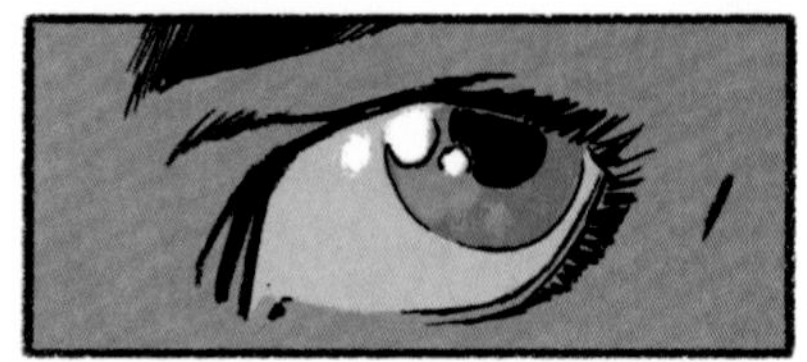

I wanted to tell him how grateful I was.

But his look stopped me.

And then suddenly...

EXCUSE ME, GOTTA...GET A DRINK.
He was gone.

He left us alone for hours.

While everyone buzzed around him.

THERE YOU ARE.

YOU ARE TOO BEAUTIFUL TO LOOK THAT LONELY.

MASON!
BEEN LOOKING FOR YOU AND ADELE EVERYWHERE. YOU REALLY DO LOOK...
JUST SLIGHTLY EXTRA STUNNING.

SO, HOW ARE THINGS? HE BEEN BEHAVING BETTER?

YES, THEN NO, THEN YES, AND NOW, NO.

YOU REALLY DON'T HAVE TO TALK TO ME. I'M SURE THERE ARE MORE IMPORTANT PEOPLE HERE.
SOMEONE YOU SHOULD BE TALKING TO?

YOU MEAN ALL THESE PHONIES? I'D RATHER HAVE A COOKIE WITH YOU AND MY NIECE ANY DAY.

IF ISABEL WAS ANYTHING LIKE HER BROTHER, ROCHESTER WAS A LUCKY MAN.
UNCLE MASON!

MY DARLING, ADELE! DID YOU ENJOY THE BALLET?
OH YES! I LOVE THE POOFY SKIRTS.
DO YOU WANT A COOKIE?

Suddenly, I felt eyes on me.

JANE, ADELE ASKED YOU IF YOU WANTED A COOKIE.
OH, SORRY... SURE.

Then Rochester disappeared again, until...

SO, YOU AND MASON ARE GOOD FRIENDS. I HAD NO IDEA.

HE'S ADELE'S UNCLE. YOUR PARTNER. I MET HIM AT THE APARTMENT.

YOU'VE DONE MORE THAN MEET HIM. ANYONE CAN SEE THAT.

YOU'RE OUT OF LINE. I'M GETTING ADELE AND WE'RE GOING HOME.

I KNOW HE'S CHARMING, BUT HE'S DATED EVERY ELIGIBLE WOMAN IN TOWN.
I'M NOT HAVING THIS CONVERSATION WITH YOU.

KRSSSH

DON'T YOU DARE TOUCH ME RIGHT NOW. IT'S TIME TO GO.

FINE. GO, THEN.

CLICK

WHAT IS **WRONG** WITH YOU? WHY DID YOU ACT LIKE THAT BACK THERE?

FINE, I'M GOING HOME.

PLEASE. DON'T GO.

I WAS A JERK, I DRANK TOO MUCH... JUST DON'T GO.

PLEASE.

YOU WERE VERY RUDE.

I WAS JEALOUS.

MASON IS CHARMING. EVERYONE LOVES HIM. THEY ALWAYS HAVE.

I'M NOT LIKE THAT. NEVER HAVE BEEN. SOMETIMES IT BOTHERS ME.

THANK YOU FOR SAYING THAT.

...I'VE NEVER LIKED PARTIES. I'M CRAP AT PARTIES.
YOU? I DIDN'T NOTICE.
ISABEL IS THE CHARMING ONE. I MEAN, WAS.

THERE WAS ONLY ONE THING I WANTED TO DO AT THAT STUPID PARTY.
DANCE.

REALLY? WITH WHO?

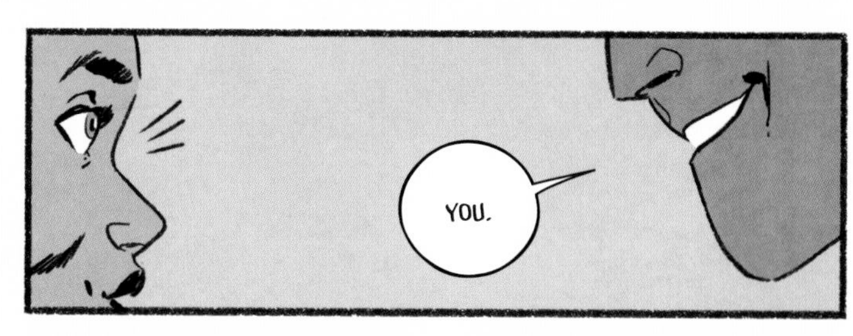
YOU.

DANCE, LIKE...

YES, EXACTLY.

YOU'RE BEAUTIFUL. YOU DO KNOW THAT, RIGHT?

OH, THAT'S RIDICULOUS.
NO, IT ISN'T.

I KNOW WHAT I AM. OKAY FROM CERTAIN ANGLES. BUT NICE OF YOU TO SAY. THANK YOU.

FOR A DANCE.
YOU KNOW WHAT? MAYBE HERE IS BETTER ANYWAY.

ARE YOU STILL MAD AT ME?
HMMM... LEMME THINK.

I...CAN'T... REMEMBER...

LET'S GO.
WHAT?

COME ON.
COME ON *WHERE?*

I HAVE AN IDEA.

HMM... IT'S SUPPOSED TO BE AT ONE OF THESE DOCKS.

YOU HAVE A BOAT?

THAT'S WHAT THEY TELL ME. YOU KNOW HOW TO DRIVE ONE OF THESE THINGS, RIGHT?

Yeah. I did.

BEEN SO LONG SINCE I SAW A HORIZON. I USED TO SEE IT EVERY DAY. IT'S HOW I KNEW WHERE I WAS.

YOU KNOW, WHEN YOU DRAW, THE HORIZON IS EVERYTHING.

LOOK AT MY HAND. IT'S CLOSE TO YOU, IT LOOKS HUGE. THE HORIZON TELLS YOU HOW BIG THINGS NEED TO BE.

PEOPLE THINK IT'S EASY TO DRAW THINGS THE WAY THEY ARE. BUT IT ISN'T. YOU HAVE TO LEARN HOW TO SEE THINGS CLEARLY. AND THAT'S NOT EASY.
AH, I'M SORRY. AM I BORING YOU?
NO.

IT'S FASCINATING, JUST LIKE YOU.

LET'S FORGET EVERYTHING FOR A SECOND, OKAY? EVERYTHING. THE WHOLE WORLD.

EVERYONE BUT US.

WHEN YOU LOSE SOMEONE YOU LOVE, A LIGHT GOES OUT.

YOU LEARN TO FIND YOUR WAY WITHOUT IT.

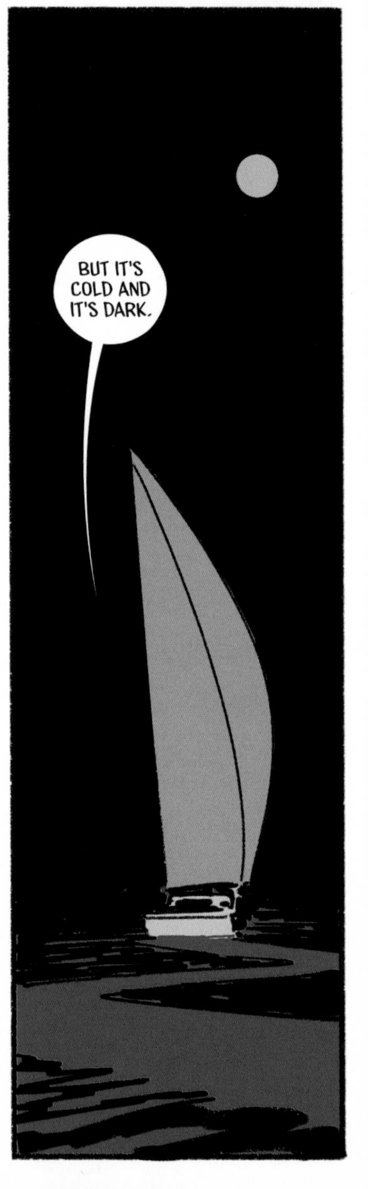
BUT IT'S COLD AND IT'S DARK.

I knew how he felt. I'd had my fair share of loss.

And for a moment, we had found a different kind of light.

A light that shone on our funny little family for weeks.
Until one awful day.
HE'S GONE.
ADELE, WHERE'S YOUR FATHER?
HE LEFT, AGAIN.

MAYBE HE WILL BE BACK SOON. WE'LL MAKE HIM A WELCOME HOME BANNER.
YOU DON'T UNDERSTAND. WHEN HE GOES AWAY, HE'S GONE FOR A LONG TIME.

STEVE, WHERE IS HE? TELL ME. I DESERVE TO KNOW.

THIS IS CRAZY.
HE SHOULD AT LEAST HAVE SAID GOODBYE TO ADELE.

HE LEFT YOU A NOTE.
A... NOTE?

DING

MASON, THIS IS *RIDICULOUS.*

HE WANTS ME TO STAY WITH ADELE AT HIS APARTMENT WHILE HE'S GONE. WHAT DOES HE EXPECT? THAT I'LL JUST DROP EVERYTHING AND...
JANE, I KNOW THAT--
DO YOU KNOW WHERE HE IS?
HE'S IN ASIA. FOR WORK. HE VOLUNTEERED TO LEAVE.

HE... VOLUNTEERED TO LEAVE?
YES, SORRY. HE'S LIKE THAT.

GREAT, SO I'M SUPPOSED TO JUST HANG OUT WITH ADELE, MAGDA, AND THE MAN WHO GOES UPSTAIRS?
WHAT MAN?
SIGH
NEVER MIND.

I'M VERY SORRY, JANE.

"IF YOU DECIDE TO QUIT, NO ONE WILL BLAME YOU."
WHERE IS JANE?
TIME FOR BED.
WAIT. JUST WAIT.

BING

I KNEW YOU WOULD COME. I KNEW IT, I KNEW IT.

GUESS WE'RE GONNA BE ROOMIES FOR A WHILE, MAGDA.

Days went by...

Then weeks.

Then months.

I tried to keep Adele's mind off her father.

And it worked.

But I kept thinking about him. I tried to hide that from her.

YOU GUYS GOING OUT TONIGHT?

YEP. WANNA COME?

These were people my age. And this was not a gloomy mansion.

I should have been having fun.

YOU OKAY?

OH, YEAH. FINE.
But I wasn't.

I just kept wondering...

When would he be back?

FWOOSH

Suddenly, an echoing sound from the hallway.

HAHAHAH
HUH?

AH, FINALLY...

He was back, but not alone.

SO THIS IS THE MYSTERIOUS MANSION PEOPLE TALK ABOUT.

YOU KNOW, PEOPLE THINK YOU'RE QUITE THE ENIGMA.
HA HA.

YOU SHOULD MEET ADELE. I'LL HAVE THE NANNY BRING HER.

A NANNY? SHOULD I BE JEALOUS?
HA HA. NO.

OH, JANE. THERE YOU ARE.

I BROUGHT ADELE SOME PRESENTS FROM MY TRIP. CAN YOU BRING HER IN?

OF COURSE.

ELIZA HELPED TO PICK THESE THINGS OUT IN TAIPEI.
THESE ARE VERY NICE EVEN THOUGH NONE OF THEM ARE HORSES OR EVEN PONIES.

WHAT'S SO FUNNY?

NUDGE
ADELE...

SORRY. I MEAN, THANK YOU.

YOU'RE WELCOME, NOW OFF TO BED. ELIZA, I WILL WALK YOU OUT.

DING

DON'T BE MAD. ELIZA...IT'S COMPLICATED. IT'S BUSINESS.
OH, I BET IT'S BUSINESS.

JANE, PLEASE.

ADELE HAS HAD HER BATH, HER HOMEWORK IS DONE...
ZZT

WHERE ARE YOU GOING?
YOU'RE BACK. YOU DON'T NEED ME LIVING HERE ANYMORE. SO I'M GOING BACK TO MY LIFE.

WAIT A SECOND.

I'M LEAVING.

JANE, WAIT.

I DON'T HAVE TO EXPLAIN MYSELF TO YOU. WHERE I GO, WHO I'M WITH--
THAT'S RIGHT. YOU DON'T.

BECAUSE WHAT HAPPENED BETWEEN US... IT WAS NOTHING. YOU'VE MADE THAT VERY CLEAR.

I GET IT. I'M POOR AND INVISIBLE, YOU CAN DO WHAT YOU WANT, IS THAT IT?

WHY DID YOU JUST DISAPPEAR? WHY ARE THINGS THE WAY THEY ARE AROUND HERE? WHAT'S ON THE THIRD FLOOR?
THOSE THINGS I CAN'T TELL YOU.
YOU **ABANDONED** ADELE. DO YOU UNDERSTAND WHAT THAT DOES TO A KID? I DO. I KNOW WHAT IT'S LIKE TO FEEL ALONE IN THE WORLD--

JANE!

IF YOU JUST CALM DOWN. THAT WOMAN WAS NOT WHAT YOU THINK--

I CAME BACK... SOONER THAN I SHOULD HAVE FOR YOU. I'M HERE NOW.

TALK TO ME...

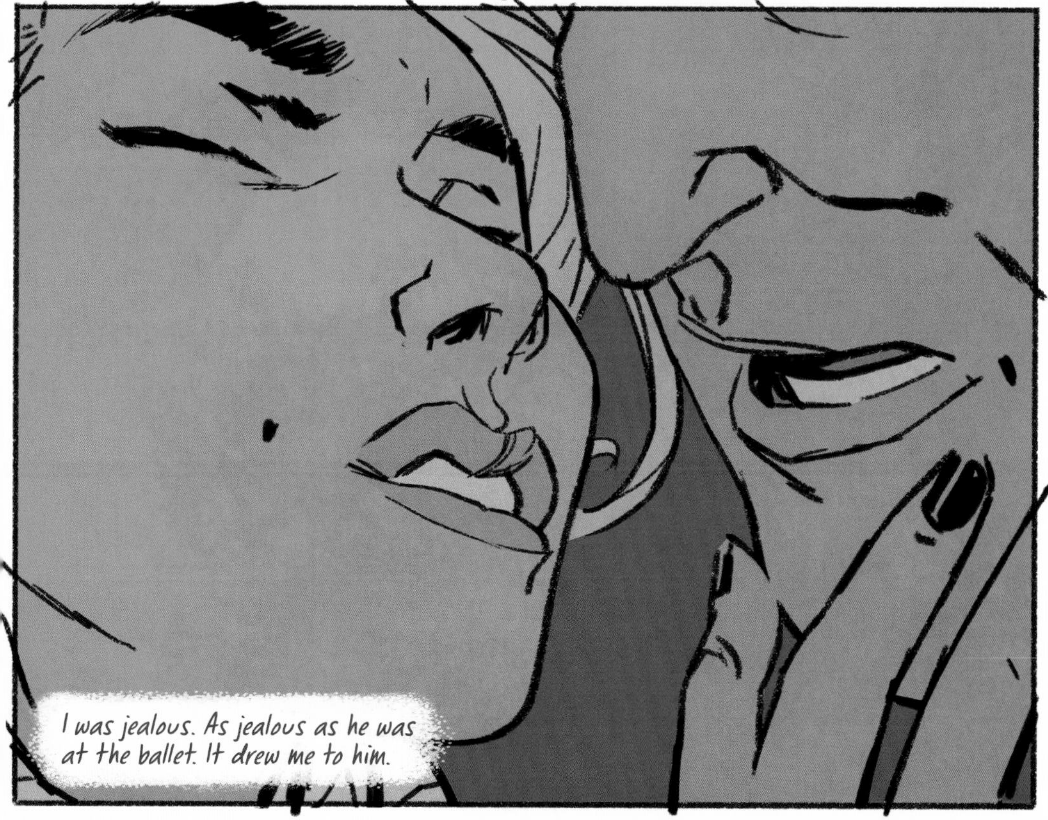
I was jealous. As jealous as he was at the ballet. It drew me to him.

NO.
JANE--
I NEED TO KNOW WHAT YOU ARE. WHO YOU ARE. THERE CAN'T BE SECRETS.

I NEED THE TRUTH.

TOK

WHAT WAS THAT?

STAY HERE.

ROCHESTER!
UHHRGH

HURRY, GET THE BODYGUARD!
BUT...

KRAK
HELP HIM!

I'LL GET ADELE.

CLIK

UPSTAIRS. NOW.

CREAK

TOSS
TRIP

OOF!
THUD

GET OFF!

KLOK

YOU SAVED MY LIFE...

ARE THEY GONE?
YES, THEY'RE ALL GONE. ROCHESTER IS WITH ADELE. I'LL DO A FULL SWEEP.

...BEN. MY NAME IS BEN.

Suddenly I was alone. I heard the rhythmic hum from upstairs.
THRUM
THRUM

THRUM THRUM
THRUM THRUM

THRUM
THRUM

THRUM
THRUM
I should have run for my life, but the sound drew me forward.

THRUM

THRUM
THRUM

THRUM
THRUM

CL'K

THRUM
I knew somehow the answer was here.

THRUM
THRUM

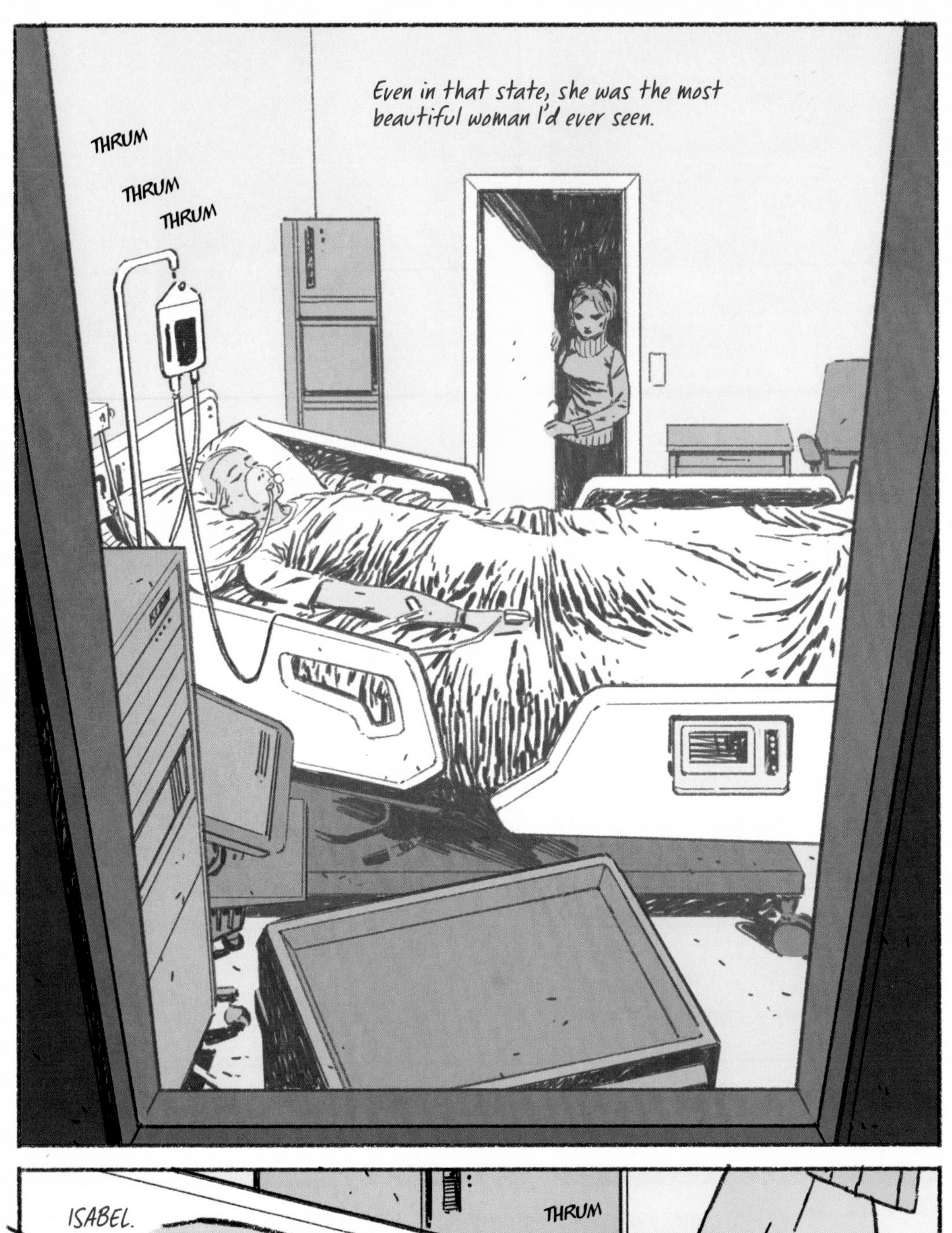
THRUM
THRUM
THRUM
Even in that state, she was the most beautiful woman I'd ever seen.

ISABEL.
THRUM

JANE, NO MATTER WHAT HAPPENS, YOU CAN'T TELL PEOPLE WHAT YOU SAW HERE. EVER.
THRUM
THRUM

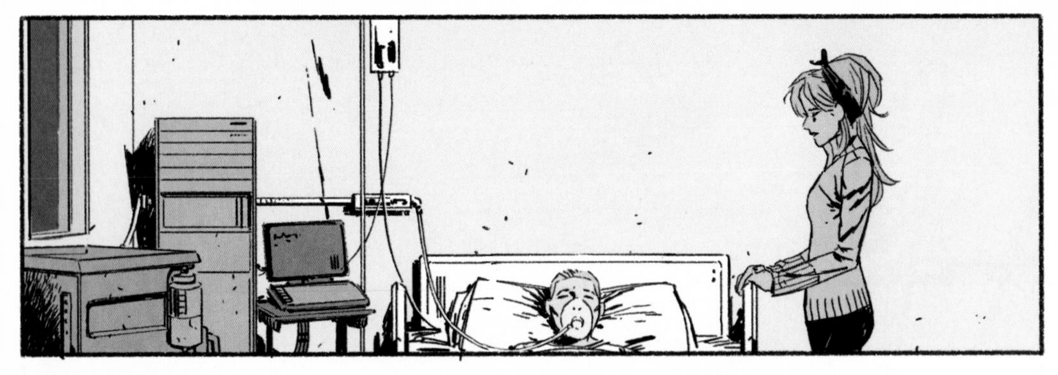

BUT... WHY?

I WILL EXPLAIN IT TO YOU. I PROMISE. BUT NOT NOW. NOW WE HAVE TO GO.

ADELE, SHE HAS NO IDEA...HER MOTHER IS RIGHT HERE

JANE--

THERE'S NO TIME, WE--

I WAS FALLING IN LOVE WITH YOU. YOU WERE LETTING ME.

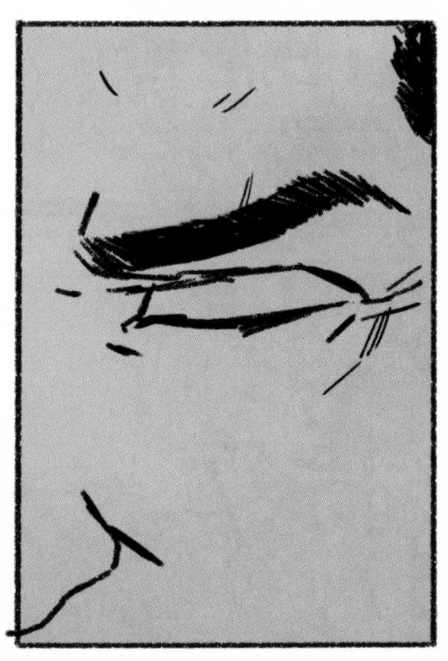

SIR, THE HELICOPTER IS READY. WE NEED TO GO. **NOW.**

GO?

ISABEL GOES FIRST, SO ADELE DOESN'T SEE HER. ONCE SHE'S GONE, WE FOLLOW.

WHUP WHUP WHUP
COME WITH US. I CAN KEEP YOU SAFE, BUT ONLY IF YOU GO WITH ME--

GO **WITH** YOU--

YES, I KNOW IT'S A LOT TO TAKE IN RIGHT NOW...YOU JUST HAVE TO TRUST ME.
WHUP WHUP WHUP WHUP

I WANTED TO TRUST YOU. BUT ALL YOU DID WAS LIE TO ME. YOU'VE NEVER TOLD ME THE TRUTH. NOT ABOUT ANYTHING.
THERE ARE REASONS. COME WITH US. NOW.

PLEASE.

740
I couldn't go with them, I just couldn't. Not when there had been so many lies.
I wanted answers. So, I turned to someone I thought might have them...

YOU ARE RIGHT. YOU DESERVE THE TRUTH.
SINCE ISABEL'S DEATH, HE'S CHANGED.

OBSESSED WITH WORK, ALWAYS TRAVELING.
I WAS AFRAID HE HAD GOTTEN MIXED UP IN SOMETHING SHADY.
AND I GUESS I WAS RIGHT.

IS THERE ANYTHING YOU CAN TELL ME ABOUT WHERE THEY WENT? ADELE IS MY FAMILY, I LOVE HER, JUST LIKE YOU DO. SHE MIGHT BE IN DANGER.

I--I'M SORRY. I DON'T. I DON'T KNOW ANYTHING.

I SHOULD GO. THANK YOU FOR... FOR ALWAYS BEING THERE FOR ME, MASON.

SHE SAYS SHE DOESN'T KNOW ANYTHING.

CLIK
CLACK

HEY! YOU'RE BACK!

JANE? YOU OKAY?
I DON'T KNOW.
FWUMP

Adele's mother was alive. She didn't know.

RIIIP
Mason's sister was alive.

CRUNCH

But I had kept Rochester's promise and said nothing.

I was still loyal to him. Why?

WHICH ONES ARE YOU SUBMITTING?

TO THE SHOW.

OH, NOTHING. CHANTAL HATES MY WORK.
DING
YOU'RE CRAZY. I LOVE YOUR WORK. IT'S REAL. AND SAD.

I looked at my phone. A text from Adele.
SKRITCH

JANE, WHAT'S WRONG? WHERE ARE YOU GOING?
I GOTTA RUN.

NOW.

ARE YOU SURE YOU WANT TO DO THIS?
HECTOR, I HAVE TO GO SEE HER. HER TEXT SAID "PLEASE COME FIND ME. WE NEED YOU. WE ARE HERE..."

"'ON AN ISLAND SHAPED LIKE A STAR.' I KNOW THAT ISLAND, HECTOR. THERE'S A HUGE MANSION ON IT, YOU CAN SEE IT FROM THE SEA.

"I HAVE TO GO TO ADELE. SHE NEEDS ME.

VROOO
OOSH

VRMM

"I'LL FIND HER AND BRING HER HOME."

I wound my way North, through the same streets that led me to New York not so long ago.

I chartered a boat and sailed on the waters I knew so well...

Headed to a lonely house on a deserted island.

BEN! DON'T SHOOT!

IT'S ME! JANE.

WHERE IS ADELE?
IN THE HOUSE. POWER'S OUT. BE CAREFUL.

JANE IS HERE, SIR.

JANE?

HURRY.

HOW DID YOU FIND US?
YOU MIGHT WANT TO HIDE YOUR IPAD A LITTLE BETTER. WHAT'S GOING ON?

HIDING AND RUNNING AWAY WON'T FIX YOUR PROBLEMS, ROCHESTER.

I WANT TO HELP YOU AND ADELE, BUT I NEED TO KNOW THE TRUTH FIRST.

ROCHESTER, WHY DOESN'T MASON KNOW HIS SISTER IS STILL ALIVE?

WHY DOESN'T ADELE KNOW?

BECAUSE NO ONE COULD. THAT'S WHAT THOSE BUSINESS TRIPS I TAKE ARE ABOUT, JANE--

--FINDING OUT WHO DID THIS TO ISABEL AND WHY. HER EXISTENCE HAD TO BE A SECRET OR THEY MIGHT COME BACK TO FINISH THE JOB.

WE NEED TO GET READY TO LEAVE.

ROCHESTER, COME ON, IT'S ME. TELL ME WHAT'S GOING ON.

I SHOULDN'T HAVE GOTTEN YOU MIXED UP IN THIS.

GO HOME.

ARE YOU INVOLVED IN SOMETHING ILLEGAL? THAT'S WHAT MASON SAID.

MASON?

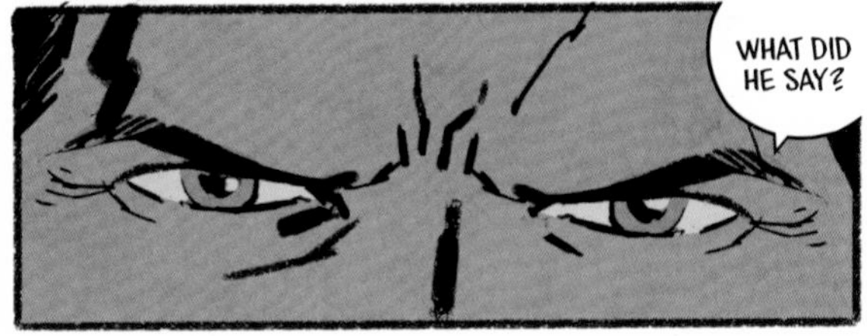
WHAT DID HE SAY?

WHO ELSE DID YOU TALK TO? DID YOU TELL ANYONE ABOUT ISABEL?

NO, BUT MASON HAS A RIGHT TO KNOW. AND SO DOES ADELE.

TELL ME WHO YOU TOLD.
I SAID NO ONE!

WHAT'S WRONG WITH YOU?

YOU'RE ACTING CRAZY.

IT'S LIKE I DON'T EVEN KNOW YOU ANYMORE.

I'M VERY SORRY, JANE.

I SHOULD NEVER HAVE LET US GET SO CLOSE. IT WAS WRONG.

IT'S ENOUGH THAT I RUINED ISABEL'S LIFE. THE MEN WHO ATTACKED HER WERE AFTER ME, DON'T YOU UNDERSTAND?

"I DON'T WANT TO RUIN YOUR LIFE TOO, JANE.

"WHOEVER CAME AFTER US IS STILL COMING. YOU NEED TO GO. PLEASE."

Somehow it had happened again.

I had found myself in another home with no room for me.

The people I loved were about to disappear.
BEN, GET THE HELICOPTER READY. WE NEED TO MOVE.

BEN!

BEN?! BEN!

JANE! STOP! SOMETHING'S WRONG. DON'T OPEN THAT DOOR.

CLICK

THANK YOU FOR LEADING US HERE.
MASON!

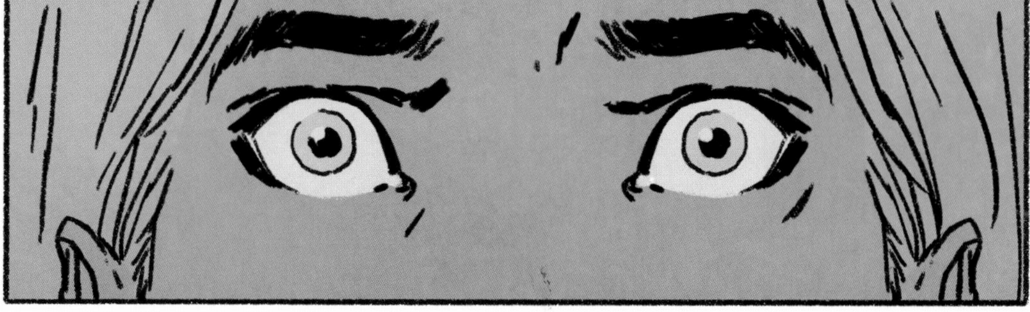

YOU FOLLOWED HER HERE. WHY?

MAGDA!
SHH... COMING, SWEETIE.

I'M SORRY, ADELE...

YOUR FATHER AND I HAVE SOMETHING TO DISCUSS.

This was not the Mason I knew. Something was very wrong.
DADDY?
GO WITH MAGDA. EVERYTHING WILL BE FINE.
MY MEN SAW ISABEL IN YOUR APARTMENT, LYING IN THAT BED...

TAKE ADELE, MAGDA, AND JANE OUTSIDE.

DON'T WORRY, ADELE.

WE'LL MAKE IT QUICK.

WHY DID YOU SEND MEN TO MY APARTMENT?

WHY DO YOU HAVE A GUN, MASON? I DON'T KNOW WHAT YOU WANT BUT YOU'RE SCARING ADELE.

DADDY, WHAT'S GOING ON?
I SAID, TAKE THEM OUTSIDE!

COME ON.

YOU STAY CLOSE TO MAGDA. BE BRAVE.
I WILL.

There was no way I was leaving Rochester alone.

FINE, COME ALONG, JANE. YOU DESERVE ANSWERS TOO.

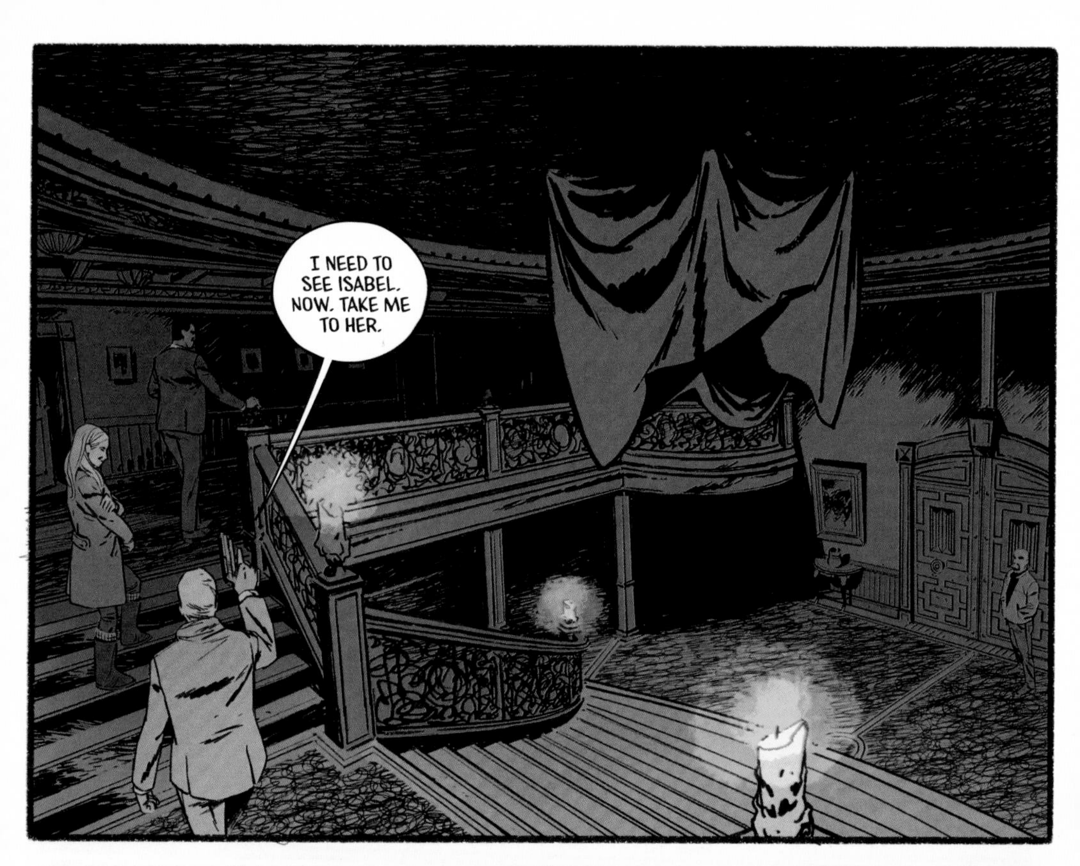
I NEED TO SEE ISABEL. NOW. TAKE ME TO HER.

WHY ARE YOU DOING THIS?

I NEED TO SEE HER. OPEN IT.

SHE'S BEEN LIKE THAT EVER SINCE THE ATTACK. SHE'S HAD THE BEST CARE.

THE DOCTORS SAID SHE HAD NO HOPE OF RECOVERY, BUT I WAITED AND WISHED AND HOPED THAT SOMEDAY THEY WOULD BRING HER BACK TO ME AND ADELE.

OH, MY POOR ISABEL.

SHE WAS THE CLOSEST PERSON TO ME, ALWAYS.

YOU NEVER UNDERSTOOD HOW MUCH I LOVED HER.

AND YOU NEVER APPRECIATED HER. SHE'S COMING WITH ME.

I WILL TAKE CARE OF HER NOW.

OVER MY DEAD BODY.

IF YOU HAD DIED LIKE YOU WERE SUPPOSED TO, NONE OF THIS WOULD HAVE HAPPENED!

THE PLAN WAS FOR YOU TO DIE, NOT HER!

SO THAT SHE AND I COULD BE TOGETHER. AND I COULD FINALLY TELL HER I LOVED HER.

SHE GOT IN THE WAY OF A BULLET MEANT FOR YOU.

SHE ALWAYS LOVED ME BEST UNTIL YOU CAME ALONG.
TOK
WELL, NOW SHE'S MINE.
YOU'RE SICK. YOU ARE HER BROTHER.
SHUT UP! YOU KEPT ME FROM HER. SHE NEVER KNEW HOW I FELT ABOUT HER, NOW SHE WILL!

JANE!

KRAK

SKIT

SKAT

ARE YOU OKAY?

DRIP

LET'S GET ISABEL OUT OF HERE.

SHE STAYS WITH ME!

KRAK

IF I CAN'T HAVE HER, NO ONE CAN.
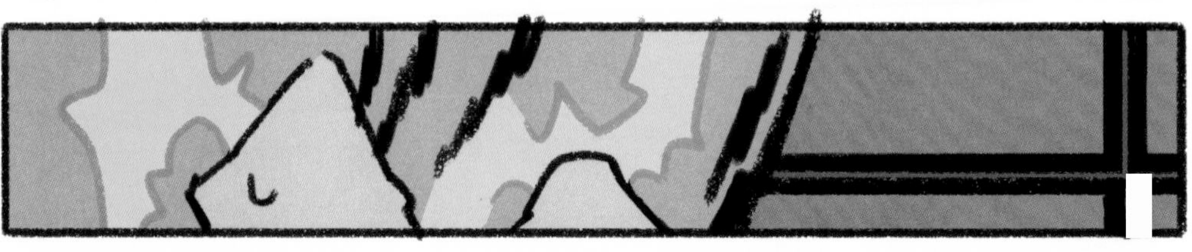

YOU'VE LOST YOUR MIND!

FWOOSH

As the two men battled, Isabel lay silent, forgotten.

KRAK

YOU ARE NEVER GOING TO HURT ISABEL AGAIN!
KRAK

KRASH

KRAK

CRASH

Isabel meant everything to Rochester and Adele. I couldn't leave her alone. It would have been soulless and heartless.

DADDY?

A-ADELE...
SWEETIE...

SIR, ARE YOU ALL RIGHT?

WHERE IS ISABEL? WHERE IS JANE?

COUGH
COUGH

JANE!
MOMMY?
PLOF
I TRIED. I COULDN'T SAVE HER.
I'M SO SORRY, I COULDN'T SAVE HER.

EARTH TO JANE...

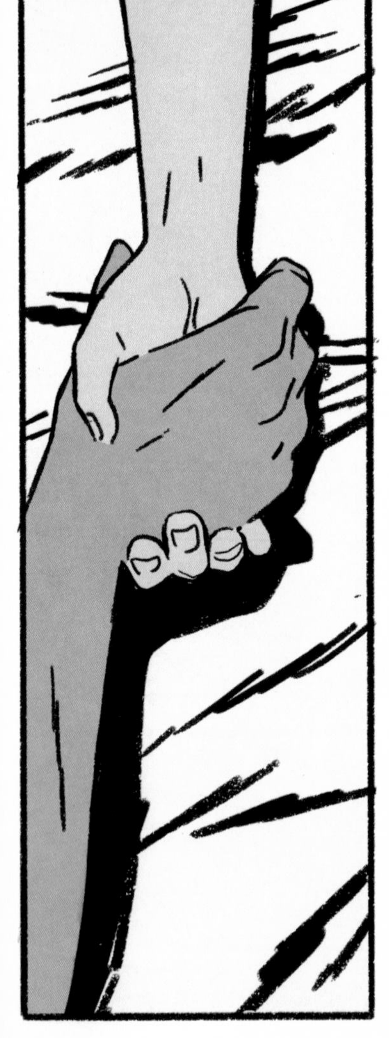

...HECTOR...

I HEAR YOU HAD A HARROWING EXPERIENCE, YOUNG LADY...
YOU COULD SAY THAT.

THANKS FOR BEING HERE, MY FRIEND.

DOCTOR SAID YOU SHOULD BE DEAD.
WHICH WOULD HAVE BEEN A BUMMER BECAUSE WHO ELSE WOULD PAY TO SLEEP WITH MY CANNED GOODS?

CTV2
..RICHARD MASON DIED AT THE SCENE, AS DID AN UNIDENTIFIED WOMAN. WE'LL PROVIDE MORE DETAILS AS THE STORY DEVELOPS.

SO SORRY TO HEAR ABOUT WHAT HAPPENED. HAVE YOU HEARD FROM ADELE?

SHE HAS BEEN THROUGH SO MUCH, LOST SO MUCH... I WANT TO GIVE HER SOME TIME.

JANE, I LOOKED AT YOUR WORK. YOU SURPRISED ME.

HAVE YOUR PIECES TO THE GALLERY BY FRIDAY.
YOU'RE IN THE SHOW.

WELCOME TO THE BIG CITY, BABY! YOU'RE IN!

SO, WHAT DO YOU THINK?
ACCEPTABLE. NICE.

HAR HAR. LET'S GO.

I'M IMPRESSED, FISH GIRL.

ISN'T THIS INCREDIBLE?! WHAT A GREAT SHOW.
YEAH, NOT BAD.

SO PROUD OF US.

WHAT'S NEXT FOR YOU, MS. EYRE?
TAP TAP

HI! DID YOU MISS ME?

ADELE!

CAN YOU SHOW ME AROUND?

IT'LL COST YOU.

JANE.

YOU'RE... HERE.
NOWHERE ELSE WE'D RATHER BE.
37

TELL ME MORE ABOUT THESE PAINTINGS.
OKAY, YOU BET...
RKP

MY PARENTS WORKED ON THE WATER.
ONE DAY, THEY WENT OUT TO SEA...AND THEY DIDN'T COME BACK.
fin
PAREL 2017.

About the Author

Aline Brosh McKenna is an award-winning filmmaker and one of the highest-grossing female screenwriters of all time. McKenna is best known for the film adaptation of the popular novel, "The Devil Wears Prada." The screenplay is considered a modern classic, filled with memorable and oft-quoted lines, and features one of Meryl Streep's signature roles as the imperious magazine editor, Miranda Priestly. In 2006, McKenna garnered Writers Guild, BAFTA and Scripter award nominations for the worldwide box office hit.

In 2014, McKenna added television to her resume when she co-created the critically acclaimed, Emmy Award-winning CW series, "Crazy Ex-Girlfriend." As Showrunner, Head Writer and Executive Producer since its inception, she is currently leading the program into its third season. McKenna also directed the Season 1 finale, and directed and wrote the Season 2 finale of the show. She created the series with its star, Rachel Bloom.

McKenna's feature film credits include the worldwide hit and perennial wedding favorite, "27 Dresses," starring Katherine Heigl; "Morning Glory," starring Rachel McAdams and Harrison Ford; the Cameron Crowe-directed, Matt Damon-starrer, "We Bought a Zoo;" and her adaptation of the musical "Annie," which was acclaimed for its diverse cast and unique approach to updating the Broadway classic.

About the Artist

Ramón K. Pérez is the multiple Eisner and Harvey Award winning cartoonist best known for his graphic novel adaptation of *Jim Henson's Tale Of Sand*. Other lauded sequential works include *Nova, All-New Hawkeye, The Amazing Spider-Man: Learning To Crawl, John Carter: The Gods Of Mars, Wolverine & the X-Men*, and creator owned endeavours *Butternutsquash* and *Kukuburi*. Outside of comics, Ramón's work can be found in Classic RPG's and CCG's, and in various editorial, book, and advertising illustration. Ramón resides in Toronto, in a horse house, with his three plants and Boba Fett.

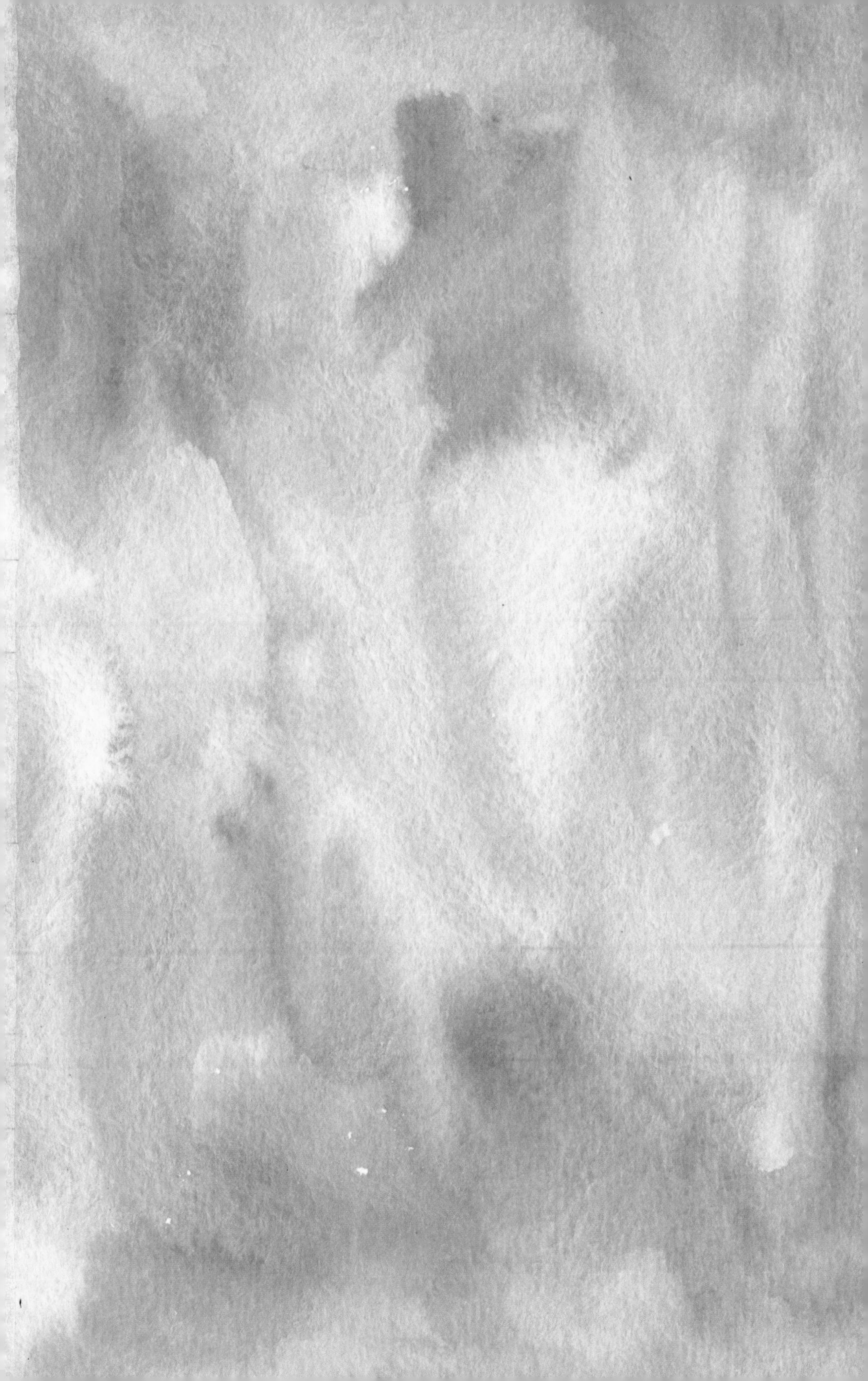